THIS *SWEET PICKLES®* **BOOK BELONGS TO**

In the world of *Sweet Pickles,* each animal gets into a pickle because of an all too human personality trait.

This book is about Bashful Bear who is so shy he's afraid to try almost everything.

Books in the Sweet Pickles Series:

Library of Congress Cataloging in Publication Data

Reinach, Jacquelyn.
  Scaredy bear.

  (Sweet Pickles series)
  SUMMARY: Bear really wants to be friends with
Pig, but is so bashful he can't figure out how to
do it.
  [1. Bears—Fiction. 2. Pigs—Fiction.
3. Friendship—Fiction] I. Hefter, Richard.
II. Title. III. Series.
PZ7.R2747Sc   [E]   78-16814
ISBN 0-03-042021-0

Copyright © 1978 Euphrosyne, Incorporated

All rights reserved, including the right to reproduce
this book or portions thereof in any form.
Published simultaneously in Canada by Holt, Rinehart
and Winston of Canada, Limited.

SWEET PICKLES is the registered trademark of
Perle/Reinach/Hefter.

Printed in the United States of America

Weekly Reader Books' Edition

Weekly Reader Books presents

SCAREDY
BEAR

Written by Jacquelyn Reinach
Illustrated by Richard Hefter
Edited by Ruth Lerner Perle

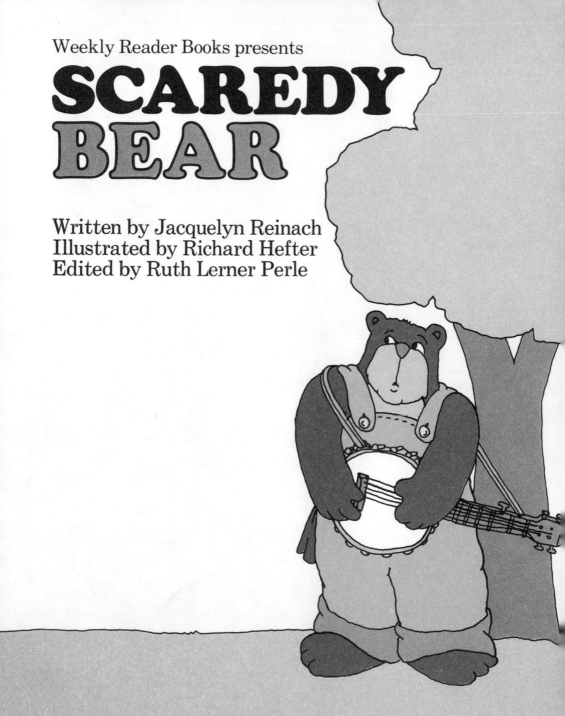

Holt, Rinehart and Winston · New York

Bear was sitting under a tree in the park one Saturday, strumming softly on his banjo. Elephant sat on a bench nearby, eating peanut butter sandwiches and humming along.

Just then, Pig came skipping happily up the path, swinging her piccolo case and bouncing a small pink ball.

Bear played a little louder so Pig would notice him, but just then Hippo came running up. Pig shot the ball to Hippo. Hippo made a perfect catch, and the two of them ran off laughing toward the playground.

Bear sighed and stopped playing.

"What's the matter?" called Elephant.

"Pig is always laughing and having so much fun," said Bear. "I wish I could be friends with her!"

"Pig seems pretty friendly to everybody," said Elephant munching a carrot.

"But I'd like her to be my *special* friend," said Bear. "Someone to play with, or . . . " and he sighed a bigger sigh, "someone to come over to my house and play duets. I could play my banjo and Pig could play her piccolo! We could make beautiful music together!"

"Well," said Elephant, "why don't you just ask her?"

"Uh....uh...," Bear gulped. "Uh...no. I couldn't do that."

"But why not?" insisted Elephant, peeling a banana.

"Well . . . uh . . . well, she's never asked *me*!" said Bear.

"She probably doesn't know you want to be friends with her," said Elephant. "Nobody knows!"

"Why is that?" asked Bear.

"Because you never talk to anybody," said Elephant. "You're always sitting all by yourself. Alligator and Kangaroo think you're stuck up!"

"Stuck up! Oh, no! I just can't think of what to say to anybody!"

"Well, maybe if you tell Pig how you feel," said Elephant, "then everybody will know you're really friendly."

Bear hung his head and shuddered. "But what if I ask Pig to be friends and she says, 'No!'?"

"Pig wouldn't do that," yawned Elephant, closing her eyes.

"Listen, Elephant," said Bear. "You're always having lunch with Pig. Why don't *you* mention to her that I'd like to be friends?"

Elephant didn't answer. She was fast asleep.

"Oh, well," sighed Bear. Then he slung his banjo over his shoulder and left the park.

On his way home, Bear saw a sign on a telephone booth. *Call A Friend Today*, it said.

"Oh!" said Bear. "Maybe I could try that. Maybe I could."
Bear went into the telephone booth. He took a coin out of his pocket and dropped it in the slot.

He dialed Pig's number.

The telephone rang.

"Maybe she won't be home," he thought, as he heard the telephone ringing.

The telephone rang again. "Maybe she's still in the park," said Bear.

The telephone rang a third time. "Maybe she's doing something and I'm disturbing her," he groaned.

Then Bear heard the receiver being picked up and Pig's cheerful voice saying, "Hello!"

Bear's heart began to pound.
"Hello!" said Pig again.

Bear's knees began to shake.
"Hello! Is somebody there?" asked Pig.
"No!" cried Bear, and hung up.

Bear's heart was pounding and he had a funny feeling in
his stomach. He sat down on the curb and held his head.
Tears began to splash out of his eyes onto the sidewalk.

Just then, Zebra and Alligator and Kangaroo came out of the park. When Zebra saw Bear, he waved and zipped across the street. Alligator and Kangaroo followed.

Bear rubbed his eyes and pretended to be watching the traffic.

Zebra came up and smiled. "I've been wanting to tell you I like your banjo playing," said Zebra.
"Oh?" said Bear.

"Yes," continued Zebra, "I like your banjo playing and so does Pig!"

"PIG likes my banjo playing!" cried Bear. "How do you know that?"

"She said so in the park this morning," said Zebra. "And she told Alligator and Kangaroo, too!"

"Oh, my!" said Bear. He smiled a little smile and blushed.

"I think Pig would like to play a duet with you," smiled Zebra. "You could play your banjo and she could play her piccolo."

"She wanted to call you," said Kangaroo, "but your telephone number isn't listed in the directory."

"Oh, my, my, my!" said Bear again.

"Well, how about it?" asked Zebra. "Will you play a duet with Pig? We were thinking it might be fun to put on a little show."

"A *show?*" cried Bear. "With an audience? And everybody watching?"

"Yes," said Zebra. "I might even play my drum."

Bear looked at Zebra and Alligator and Kangaroo. His heart began to pound. His knees began to shake. "Excuse me," said Bear. "But I don't think I can be in a show. I am very busy, you know. And I wouldn't have the time to practice. And, uh...I'm not feeling very well!"

Bear stood up and said in a hoarse voice, "Please tell Pig
I'm sorry but I can't do it." Then Bear picked up his
banjo and shuffled away.

Weekly Reader Books offers several exciting
card and activity programs. For information,
write to WEEKLY READER BOOKS, P.O. Box 16636,
Columbus, Ohio 43216.

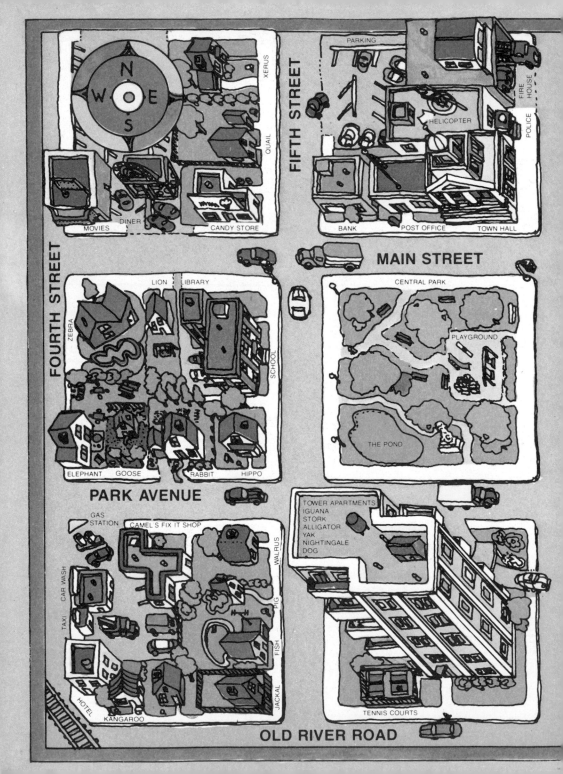